NOSTALGIC DEMENTIA

ABHIDHRUV

Dedicated To Darsh

Contents

Foreword

This book, is my first. It's puropse is to deliver the message of togetherness, and the everlasting symbol of underlying trust in the very hearts of every living being.

This moral is partially engulfed by a hint of mystery, suspense, along with paving the way for a clear ending. The novel's only aim, is to instill curiosity in the minds of the readers, and to show them the true meaning of an everlasting bond.

There are only a few instances of violance in the novel, however, I would recommend it to slightly matured readers, above the age of eleven.

This novel should be read with an open mind, for there are a few instances of logic, which were deliberately hidden, to provide more suspense.

I enthusiastically look forward to your responses.

Preface

This book was inspired from one of the daily newspaper clippings, which caught my eye.

A simple piece of news was modified into a thriller with an emotional message, which is to be understood by every human on the planet.

The names mentioned, are not inspired from any real-life celebrities, and are only limited to the science of fiction.

The main plot of the novel was designed in the year 2022. Trust me, you will not find it as a piece of outdated work.

As you head into this book, I hope that it grasps your attention, from the first page to the last.

Acknowledgements

I would like to thank my dear friends, family, and my close aquaintances, who have given some useful insights, which I have put in this book.

My editor, Atharv, who has given me a good amount of useful input, and is currently writing his own book.

Along with the few other members, who have recieved the original copy of this novel, implementing ideas which have thoroughly developed this manuscript.

And finally, thanks to all the readers who have bought this novel, spending their valuable time and money on it.

Thank You.

Prologue

There he sat, in front of the bonfire, regretting his actions. Being a suspended college student, and a presumed drug addict, he had only one person to blame. The person who was being very possessive of him. Fiona. He growled and grumbled while thinking of her. He loved and despised her at the same time. He wanted to kill her, but would also die for her. He stuck his hand into the blazing flames. He wanted to punish himself for his poor judgement throughout the year. He wanted to feel the singing pain.

There she was, the blue eyes, brown hair, and the creepy smile of hers. Victor didn't know what to do. He felt uncontrollably helpless in front of her. She sat down, beside him. Immediately, he stood up, and left her alone, to take a walk in the gardens. Fiona followed. "This isn't you, Victor, we can be something else. You know, I'd always imagine a future, where we would live like the lords of the world, spending each and every second of our very existence in happiness. Join me. Be the Victor I love."

Victor responded, "No, I can't. Since the beginning, I've come here to study, graduate and live a normal life. I've experienced a ton of pain. Don't put me through further periods of sorrow." Fiona resisted, "Your father was just like you. He was my inspiration. Don't say no. Please."

Victor turned back, teary eyed. He strolled towards her, unable to look straight into Fiona's eyes. He pulled her towards him, and the sound of a piercing dagger echoed across a hundred miles. "Why? Why, Victor?", screamed Fiona. She dropped down, with her face pale. Fiona's wrist grasped on to Victor's arm, tightly. She breathed rapidly for a moment. And then, she was a lifeless carcass.

He fell to his knees, "I'm sorry, Fiona. I'm Sorry."

The sky was black, just black. The white radiation of the moonlight shined on Fiona's face, and rain started pouring down. Nature was oblivious to Victor's cries of sorrow.

Part One

Awakening

I

An Unexpected Return

The sky was pitch black, with the twinkling stars spread evenly across its surface. Victor could hear the sound of owls hooting in the distance. The trees were swaying to the beats of the wind, with the clouds looking in the state of pouring down. It was nighttime. As you might have guessed, Victor was staying at a hillside house, for he was on a vacation. He was a 29-year-old youngster, with ocean-blue eyes and chocolate-brown hair. He was thin but tall, and looked like the guy who was capable enough to compete against Usain Bolt in the olympics. He was pale white, which also made him look like the kind of guy you wouldn't want in your house. This rent-in temporary house was situated near the outskirts of Canada. Victor wanted to experiece a quiet, peaceful surrounding.

It had been over six years since he had been traumatized. Everywhere he went, his dark past would haunt him. He lived with his grandparents. Taking a leave from work, he wanted to retreat in a quiet location, for a couple of days. He and his mate, Ken Grover, were on this vacation together. It was their final day off work, before heading back to their respective jobs.

Little did they know that this would lead them to the beginning of a nightmare. As Victor was relishing his meal of a Scotian Lobster Roll, his phone rang. Unexpectedly, it wasn't from any of his contacts. Plus, he hadn't signed up for one of those charity fund programs that one would see down the street or through websites.

Keeping these minute details aside, Victor answered the call. "Hello, who the hell are you?", said Victor, quite annoyed by the call, for this random stranger had phoned him at eleven in the nighttime, maybe to clear out some charity fund donations, Netflix subscriptions or any other issue that mattered to them. Whatever it was, couldn't it wait till sunrise?

The stranger at the other end started to respond, "Hello Victor. Glad to meet you again, but do you, remember me?" The stranger was a lady. Her voice was low pitched and hoarse, which made her sound like the cancer patients whom you would see at the hospital, sputtering out cheesy emotional dialogues. Listening to this woman's statement of remembering him, Victor wasn't too pleased. In fact, it was the exact opposite. Inside, he was sweating with fear, which made him shiver. His gut told him to cut the damn call and doze off right away, while Ken, the blonde guy who was eating an over-grilled Turkey Breast sandwich, suggested, "Oi, idiot, just respond! Maybe she's your long lost cousin or somethin!"

Ken was a black-eyed, blonde and bulky Canadian. Despite the fact that his origins were from Canada, he had a natural australian accent which made him look and sound like the muscular bodyguard of an influentual person.

Still shivering, Victor picked up the phone once again."Fiona?", said Victor, who was scared out of his wits. She responded, "Yes, my darling Victor, how fond I am of your sweet little voice, it makes me grin with happiness!"

Only a single question was hopping around in Victor's mind, How the frick did this psycho get his number? His fear was justified, for she was the reason of his traumatic part. The sudden memory of her disturbed him deeply. Victor's heart was beating at the speed of a motorboat.

The lady continued, "North Vancouver, Lonsdale Avenue, Stockholm apartments, Tower 9, Door number 603." For what seemed like the fifth time, Victor froze in shock, for this wasn't any ordinary address."They're watching soap operas, happily." "No! Please, don't harm them!" One phone call was disturbing Victor to the core.

"Press one, to cut off the head, press two, if you want to mutilate the body, and click three, if you are interested in planning a customized murder." Suddenly, her voice became deep; she started to laugh in the style of circus clowns."Looking forward to the main event. You'll be there, won't you?" "I'm calling the police!", Victor said; his face had started to display a blend of emotions. He looked worried, with a mind full of dispair.

"You can't, not on my watch," she replied. "I have two senior citizens in my grasp, and they are my little hostages. If you you call the police, I have two knives, an axe, and a brand new chainsaw that is waiting to be tested. Now, if you'll excuse me, I have to conduct an autopsy on two lovely oldies. But don't worry, I'll try to keep them alive for you. Until then, keep in touch."

With that statement, she cut the call. The house was nearly quiet, except the sound of Ken slurping his chicken noodles mercilessly. Victor was too scared to even cry. Somehow, his dark past had caught up to his present. After a long pause that felt like forever, Ken started to speak.

"So, how'd it go, mate?" Ken asked. Victor couldn't speak, out of fright. His lips were numb, and his vision was blurry. Moreover, his consciousness started to drift away from his mind. The very next second, he blacked out.

The second after that, he was dreaming. Victor could see flashes of his past, in the distinct shade of black and white. He wanted to shut his eyes, but he felt like he was being forced, tortured to watch the painful memories of his life. The so called telecast was on a replay. He could see a blue-eyed girl with a devilish smile, who was brutally stabbing a blurry figure with a sharp penknife repeatedly.

He felt the same clip repeating in his mind over and over again, and he couldn't stop watching. Finally, the scene started to fade, which led to the formation of another memory in his mind.

In this situation, he saw himself in a dark room, going crazy and feeling vulnerable. He could see himself hearing disturbing screams of pain and anguish, with the splattering of blood throughout the very room, and that sound could be heard from the basement. Every second of that segment of his memory convinced Victor that his life was already rotting in hell.

The next moment, the noises stopped, and the door was open, with a mysterious figure standing in its midst, as the time had come. But, once again, the scene had started to dissolve. Victor's brain had opened the doorways to his most disturbing memory yet. It was Victor himself, lying in a pool of blood, slowly succumbing to his injuries. Maybe they weren't dreams. They were probably visions of his dark future.

He was struggling from time to time, in order to leave this horrid nightmare of his. He felt a tight grasp on his left wrist, and was also smacked in the head. Finally, he was able to regain consciousness. However, he faced only a single problem.

Victor's surroundings made him a little uneasy, considering the fact that he was locked up in a calaboose. About eight to nine officers were working at the spot. Five of them wore a grey shirt and indigo trousers with matching blue overalls on the top, with a black and yellow striped hat. The overalls had coat pockets, along with a designated officer badge. They wore formal shoes, some black, some brown.The rest had nicely tucked formal shirts coloured with a bright splash of grey, with their badge attatched to the right. These officers were to be recognized by any common man as the 'RCMP', aka 'Royal Canadian Mounted Police.'

The one guy sitting at the table, about 40 - 41 years old, wearing a leather jacket, was probably the inspector. The guy was smoking two cigars at once, which made him look like a goof, rather than a dangerous super-cop from the 80's. The idiot had a 'high-but-not-too-high' pitched voice, which he used to give orders to the constables working under him. The guy was a total lunatic. Victor's eyes widened. He knew the man.

His name was Johnny Brooks. He was the officer who handled the case of Terry Jones, Victor's father, aka, a dead gangster. However, the inspector showed no familiar reaction on meeting him. Johnny acted like it was the first time he had ever seen the guy.

About several minutes later, Victor mustered up the courage to demand an explanation. "What the frick am I doing here, man?", said Victor, casually. As you might have expected, this question wasn't very well recieved.

Johnny frowned, which convinced Victor to keep his mouth shut. But anyway, the guy leapt over the table of files and stormed over to Victor's cell. "Listen up, we're the police. The RCMP. Don't even think about escaping. We'll shoot you down like the terrorists in Afghanistan."

This warning wasn't taken seriously by Victor. He wanted to know why he was in jail. He sensed that something was wrong, so he had the right to ask. "What's the damn time? Why have I been locked up? Where's Ken?." Johnny stared at him, blankly. "You sure you don't know what you've done, you rascal? Don't show me your innocence. We've obtained complete proofs at the spot. Like father, like son." Victor smirked. " Surprise me, then. What kind of a crime have I, Victor Jones, committed tonight?"

Johnny laughed. "Listen up, Kid. You've been arrested and detained as the prime suspect in the murder of your grandparents, aka Gregor and Genelia Jones."

II

Gruesome Graphic Violance

"Oh shit." After that psychotic female, aka Victor's bane, threatened him by holding his grandparents hostage, he should have been prepared for the moment. He didn't think that they would ever see the light of day, and unfortunately, he was absolutely right.

Now he was locked up in a damned cell, being mentally tortured by an inspector who surprisingly smoked two cigars at once, while frequently putting on a face that made the guy look like an african chimpanzee. To top it all, he was framed as the 'prime suspect' in the murder of his grandparents. Wonderful. Just wonderful.Victor was frozen in shock and despair. Now he could officially declare himself as an orphan and claim some donations from the rest of the world. But that wasn't really the point. Victor had a deep connection with them. He would miss it dearly. He didn't even want to prove his innocence, which made him feel completely paralyzed. It was just the usual.

"Can I see them, for once?" "Very well then. Boys?"

"But that's not part of your jurisdiction, sir", said a stout and fat constable who was serving tea to the other officers. "And who, the hell are you to remind me of my frickin' job? You are here to serve me, a mere constable. Scram, and bring me another cigar!"

As they stepped into the black Volkswagen, Victor could sense that his damned life was about to get much worse. The sun was rising, slowly, the birds chirping in a way that made Victor feel like he was being mocked at. Following a long drive, the inspector stopped at Victor's apartment. It was a bad omen.

The flat was surrounded by 'Do Not Cross' borderlines on all sides, with the door open, and the forensics team making a landfill out of his house while searching for evidence. And right in the centre, was the place where two elderly bodies were lying dead. On their sight, Victor slowly knelt towards them. They were literally unrecognizable. Kitchen knives wher pierced into the eyes mercilessly, the head was bald on both corpses, and the mouth was wide open with the tongue cut off and alternate teeth plucked out. Moreover, the hair was stuffed inside the mouth. It was gory, gruesome and a horrible sight for any kids to watch.

"Let me go! Why are you doing this to me? I'm innocent!" He shouldn't have left them at home. The more he made eye contact with the corpses, the more paranoid he felt. But this time, he wasn't going to faint, not anymore. He was going to run. Run away from this horrible nightmare of his.

He leapt across the borderline and started to run as fast as his feet could take him. The officers behind chased him; Victor couldn't stop, mainly because he had justified himself as a 'criminal on the loose' a few seconds ago. He ran and ran, till he was finally out of breath. In the middle of the woods, Victor was good as dead. He had become a wanted fugitive overnight. All he could do was hide.

He was frightened, worried and angry. No matter how fast he ran, his past would always overshadow him. Those bloody, pierced and twisted eyes were a clue to that brain of his. The past was dark and brutal, and now every aspect of his possible future would be ruined. He desperately needed a few hours of sleep to think about it all.

Victor wouldn't die as a criminal, he wouldn't die without clearing his name. To this day, fear was contollling him. The fear of his wife. The fear of his past. With his family, respect and pride gone, there was nothing more to lose. On the run, anything could go wrong. But Victor just wasn't scared. Till his final breath, Victor would stalk chase and hunt each and every idiotic psycho who played a role in his miserable life. This time, he would casually stroll towards the danger ahead and stab it right in the face, least expected.

But right now he was lost. Begging for survival. Nothing more than an abandoned baby wandering right in the middle of the jungle. The trees were swaying, its leaves were rustling, the birds were chirping, yet the forest was nearly silent, in the daytime.

On a bright summer morning, filled with positivity, Victor was frequently cursing himself as usual, due to the perfectly placed shortcomings in his partially peaceful life. With his legs hurting, along with a mentally weak will to survive, Victor tried to put himself at ease by narrating stories about ghost lizards and barbie demons and all that shit your mom would tell you if you ever misbehaved. Basically, he was talking to himself. He was going crazy, due to a lack of a proper verbal communication with anyone else. If only he had a family to help him deal with this. No.

He needed a psychiatrist. A therapist.

This reaction was probably due to the current situation of his. It was the bloody, naked truth. He couldn't bear the mental pain that he had been through. His clothes were torn amd smelly following his small stay with the RCMP. He sat down, with his back rested against a tree. He groaned.

Victor's eyes were wrinkly, and the dark circles had slowly spread across his face, like a plague or disease. His mind had recently been experiencing hallucinations, draining his mental strength almost instantly. He took out his wallet and unfolded an archaic slip of paper, which consisted of three faces; they were bright, lovely and a hint of innocence was seen in their eyes. Victor forced a smile across his dusty face, and tore the picture to shreds. He wanted to start a new life. Once more. This time, he would try to prevent all the mistake that he had done in the past, in order to keep his family safe. If only he could go back to the way things actually were. Quiet and peaceful. Everyday, filled with happiness. A life, without sadness or despair.

Victor was bleeding, mentally. It was nearly impossible to determine the presence of his very conciousness. He dozed off slowly, for a few moments, trying to recall the few but amazing memories he had, before someone had wrecked his life. It helped him deal with the present situation a bit, taking his mind off all the problems. However, this desicion made him spiral into further chaos.

Victor's wrinkled eyes struggled to stretch wide open. But one glimpse of his surroundings made him want to doze off one more time. It was the RCMP. Again. To make it worse, the psychotic cigar-smoking inspector was present. About 10 of them were cornering him. This time, he couldn't escape. They were also armed with tazers or guns. He really wished not to get electrocuted. Victor slowly raised his arms, kneeling down. "I'm all yours now," said he. "Take me to the lockup. But let me call my lawyer." Johnny chuckled, "Oh, we're not taking you to the calaboose. Think again. It's time to pay your home another long visit."

III

The Ruffians' Mansion

The name felt like it was mocking its prisoners. He failed to convince the cops, that he had been impersonated, which led them to throw poor Victor in an asylum. Unfortunately, he had been here a few years ago, which led him to develop extreme schizophrenia. This place was negetively nostalgic.

Victor's cell was no longer than an apartment washroom, except the fact that it had all the facilities residing there. His heart was restless. Sure, he was used to violent and depressing atmospheres, but his very soul was lacking something that couldn't be significantly explained in words. He was lacking an emotion, which was the key to his happiness and despair, simultaneously. She was Victor's element of life, his only reason to give himself a chance of hope. She was his better half, whether he liked it or not.

One meal a day, Victor had to eat a meal of half-baked bread and butter, along with over-cooked meat and potatoes. A day in the mental institute felt like an eternity of negetivity. Victor would rather have been caught up in the wars of Russia and Ukraine. He had no time to think, for he was too immersed in his past, full of melodramatic memories. A week passed, since his entry. It was depressingly outrageous. He had nobody to talk to, except the wall. He never was an extrovert when it came to making friends. While he took his naps, an unknown figure was the cause of his disturbance every night. Victor had suddenly found an opening to all his desired answers.

On such a night, Victor caught a glimpse of the mysterious stranger, with a black, american hoodie. He leaped towards the bars of the prison cell, demanding an answer. "Ken. You frickin' idiot." The figure slowly replied, "Yes, I drugged your food and drink, hired men to place evidence at the crime scene, erased the CCTV footage, and dumped you right next to your poor, helpless grandparents. For about a period of 15 days and 20 hours ago, your passport was replaced with that of a divorced drunkard. I am the mastermind."

"How much did she offer? Listen, if you get me out of this shithole, I'll give you double."

Ken started to cackle like an autistic witch. "You shitty human! She promised me 2 things, which you could never have: A clean record, and a second chance at life." All pure evils were seen inside Ken's twin pupils. Slowly, he shuffled away from Victor's eyesight. Damn it.

He started banging on the iron bars loudly, causing his neighbouring inmates to spring up at the noise of trouble. Victor fell to his knees, crying in anguish. In a few moments, the prison guards dragged him to the torture cell, while Victor was crying in anguish. The torture cell was dark and gloomy. Victor begged, "H- Help me, please. Check the camera's audio and video. You'll apprehend my innocence."

He was then brought to the asylum's control room, where Victor was given the privilege of checking the footage of each and every CCTV that took place in the midnight. Surprisingly, there was no appeerence of Ken in any of the cameras. The screen displayed Victor talking to himself. "We've checked all the cameras to find the traces of an unknown visitor. We couldn't find anyone." He was dragged back to the torture cell, where he was physically and mentally drained to die. Till dawn, Victor was treated like an animal in chains, struggling to break free from his emotionally isolated boundaries. His life was no less than a typical, but intense horror movie.

Victor was bruised, more than that of an army commander. He didn't take long to regain control of his senses again. By intercepting this sudden reaction, an old but studious-looking woman kneeled down, and placed a bowl of seemingly expired crisps in his eyesight. "Who are you?", was the only question he had before gobbling up the bowl of crisps. "I am Dr. Grace Collins, A psychiatrist." Victor's eyes reddened as he scrambled to the room's corner. "Leave me alone!"

The green-eyed woman smiled, "I'll see you later, Victor.", as she left the room, ordering the guards to dump Victor back in to his cell. He had to escape. Somehow. Victor held an iron needle, and started to scratch or etch the name 'Fiona.' It was his cell after all. He could give the dull, boring walls of the prison a splash of his memories. He desparately hoped to find an opening to all his questions. The next few days were tough to handle. The guards, prisoners, everyone looked at him as if he had committed a grave crime. He obviously hadn't.

One morning, at the mess hall, all the tables were moved to the corners, and Victor was in the middle of a 'chakravyuha' of prisoners and guards [Lotus shape]. "Sit down, Victor." The so-called 'psychiatrist' was back again, this time, only to trouble him.

"Tell me about the chapters of your highly interesting life, son of Terry." "Not a chance", moaned Victor, while stuttering. He didn't want to share information of his past with an unknown outsider who was most likely to report it to the police and get him killed. Or worse, she would have him go through torture.

Grace gave a signal to one of the inmates, who charged at him like a raging bull, giving Victor the creeps. He then sprinkled an entire carton of chilli flakes on him, causing Victor to squeal. This was not the treatment that he had desired from a psychiatrist. Definitely not. "This will be our frequent routine, Victor. If I sense a bit of disobedience in you, the conequences will have to be faced. I'll try my best to not kill you in our litle session. Please, Victor. Cooperate with me."

Victor gasped slowly and continued to speak, "I was born here, in Vancouver. After the age of thirteen, my parents went missing; they were presumed dead, probably murdered. To further continue my education, I was enrolled at a boarding school in Ottawa, which was also an institute of engineering. I finished my education at the age of twenty two. Since then I have been living here, with my grandparents. Before a total nutjob brutally slaughtered them!"

Grace gave Victor another hard stare, signaling to another inmate. Victor was burnt on his back with steaming hot coal, followed by his groaning whispers. "What the frick do you want from me?"

She replied, "Poor Victor, A lie is like makeup. It can be only applied to some faces, or situations. Let me correct your statement. Your parents died when you were at an early age. You spent some time in therapy, recovering from depression. You were raised by your garndparents, studied software engineeering in Jin Maple's Institution of Excellence. Lastly, you were reprimanded and suspended for getting involved in illegal activities. Remember, Victor. Fiona Rodriguez. We can track her down and retrieve all the information we need."

VIctor's eyes widened. He hadn't heard that name in years. She was one person, who had knowingly wrecked his life, turning it into nothing less than living hell. Victor gulped. He shook his head multiple times to divert the point of discussion. She was the incarnation of death.

"Listen, Victor, You have two options. Either surrender, accept that you have killed Gregor and Genelia, and reveal Fiona's whereabouts. If not, sign this document to end your limitless pain, once and for all." Victor took a close look at the documents that were handed by Grace. "No, I'm not doing it. I don't choose either. I'm not giving you access to the vault. Die." Grace smirked, "Very well then, we will have another session tomorrow. I'll torture you to the very brink of death, but you won't die, instead, you'll beg for mercy, choosing one of the two options."

Victor stood up. "Listen Grace, I know that you're after the vault and Fiona. But you're not having any of it. None. It is my family legacy. I might be a youth, but I'm the centre of a crucial political circle over here", boasted Victor. He didn't know where Fiona was, but he hoped not to stumble into her again, in the future. She was probably out there, committing crimes. She backed Ken.

"Try all you can, Victor Jones. One day, there will come a time, where you'll have to expose yourself, to the world, and your loved ones. I'll be there to watch it, and that will be the last time you will have ever have experienced the feeling of happiness. To end our little session, we will be taking you to the court of law. You hail from a family with a criminal background, and therefore, your flat and your past will be thoroughly investigated. Get ready, you don't wanna look like a fool in front of the judge."

IV
Dawn Of The Inauspicious

"Twinkle, twinkle, little star, how I wonder what you are!" The innocent face of Rahul sparkled in the moonlight, along with his smile. His mother Lakshmi would run a hundred miles, just to see that cheeky grin of his. Thw two of them were a cute pair. It was a lovely sight, Laksmi feeding Rahul yougurt, in an open-air restaurant, while Rahul continuously interrupted her by reciting his favourite rhyme. He was the apple of her eye. However, Lakshmi had a feeling of discomfort; she brushed it away. It was a Sunday, December 17th, and it was seven o' clock in the evening. To simply describe the atmosphere of the area, it was ecstatic, mainly because of the food.

Laksmi gazed at her surroundings. She really felt uneasy. Besides, her meal and Rahul's was swept clean off the plate. Something wasn't right. A small aspect of her surrounding thoroughly endangered her. It was right on the tip of her tongue, but she hadn't thought about it till then.

As seen in the movies, right when they were about to leave, the ground, which was in perfect sync with the cups and plates on the tables, started to wobble, slightly. Rahul, who looked scared, was under the impression of being a victim of a possibly impending earthquake. So was everyone else. Probably. Adding salt to their wounds, a 'Non-graphical-maybe-nuclear' explosion took place, right under the very foundation of the restaurant. Luckily, Rahul was distanced enough from the place of the blast.

The same just simply couldn't be said for Laksmi. Her face was burnt and scarred. Her soul, though, was invisisble to the distressed cries of a 4-year-old Rahul. He was unhurt, his clothes were dirty, and he had an unclear vision of his surrounding, while coughing like a patient suffering from Stage-4 Terminal cancer.

The travelling of a few steps led him to the location of his moter's corpse. Rahul burst into tears, as he sat beside Laksmi's dead body, urging her to wake up. Finally, he calmed down, for what seemed like after an eternity. He lied down, next to her, clinging to the carcass tightly with one hand, and began to suck his thumb. The houses and markets surrounding the restaurant were depried of people, probably because a group of terrorists had entered the scene. The lives of 154 people were at stake, consisting of seven political individuals and twenty six goverment officials. The rest were ordinary citizens.

Fourteen armed men were more than enough to shut the mouths of every hostage. They had advanced guns and double-XL sized upper garments covered in a light shade of brown. Their faces and heads were covered by the same, leaving enough space for the eyes; everyone had sunglasses. The leader looked the same, but the fact that he was wrapped in a darker shade of broun made him different from the others. He walked towards a middle aged man, who had been comforting Rahul all this time, for he was found sleeping next to a dead Lakshmi. The man was a journalist, with his ID hidden under a vest, and a glowing handheld-transceiver right in his pocket, connected to the intercom of a local police station.

He snatched it, pulling it close to his mouth, and spoke loudly, in a gruff voice, "I know you can hear me, so, let me get staight to the point. I have about 150 hostages with me. I presume that you wouldn't want them to die brutally, would you? Some of them have families to care for. I would also like to remind you that I have a handful of political individuals in my very grasp."

On the other end, North Vancouver's Johnny Brooks, recieved the call. In astonishment, he grinned, surprisingly. "Where's the proof? I need the count of the people with you, and only then I can fulfil your wicked demands." The terrorist hissed, "Officer, you need proofs? I'm sorry, but this isn't child's play. The ball is in my court, and you do what I say. If I slowly burn the ankles of each and every person over here, would you care? Yes, you would. Your elected government will become an ultimate face of shame, to the public, and you would lose your damn job."

Johnny responded,"What do you want?" The unknown desperado laughed. "I have three demands. Firstly, I want you to arrange transport for me and my men. Secondly, the seized container in your custody should be under my control. Finally, I want you to release Victor Jones, from custody, and bring him to me. These are my demands, and I must not be questioned of my deeds.

Johnny knew what he had to do: Use intel to extract the truth. He sped over to the asylum in his black Volkswagen, dragged Victor out of his cell [With a legal permit of course], and brought him to the NDHQ [National Defence Headquarters], where the Defence minister resided. He dumped a collection of similar files in front of the minister, Wiley Ross.

"Sir, as you can see, there have been minimal terrorist attacks in the past decades or so. We have ongoing intel on the development of various terrorist groups and none of them have planned to invade Canada or its neighbouring countries. Clearly, it is an internal attack. The criminals involved are doing their dirty work in the guise of a terrorist. Now, we have come to their demands. They seek the parole of Victor Jones, who is quite an interesting character. He has been suffering from effective schizophrenia since birth, and is the successor of mob boss Terry Jones. He was recently arrested for the murder of his grandparents. Now, coming to the second demand, it has a very peculiar connection with Victor's illegal parole. The seized container found in Abbotsford a few years ago, containing huge amounts of cocaine, should we let it go?"

Mr Ross, who looked quite interested in the case, had come to a logical conclusion. "Victor Jones. You are the offspring of an infamous criminal. Many a officer in the Canadian department have intel on your interaction with Fiona Rodriguez, who is the boss of a dangerous drug cartel that has rapidly grown in power over the past seven years. We all know that she was presumed dead after she went missing, following the capture of the Abbotsford container. Therefore, it is highly possible, that she is the head of this 'terrorist' operation. A few months later, you married Leanne Smith, who soon called an asylum to put you in. Now, there is a common thread missing in all these stories. Would you like to fill it up, Victor?

Victor gazed towards the ceiling, continuously, for a minute. "Fiona is a threat. Not to the country, but to my family. I was stuck in the asylum because of her. As long as she is alive, I will have to keep running. She has lived a life of crime, and now wants me to join, by force. I assure you, I will not escape the premises of this country. I have a story, that is waiting for its end. I will narrate my experiences with her as you wish, but at no cost, shall I return to the asylum."

V
Marital Blues

Leanne was sick. Sick of the damned world. There she lay, on the black leather chair at the centre of her room. By that, we mean that she was lazily killing time in her bestie's garage. She was hiding from an unknown source which wanted her dead. It was probably her husband, or someone from his past, who wanted him dead. The television was playing the news, and it instantly grabbed her attention. It wasn't like she had anything better to watch, anyway.

The RCMP meet the demands of the terrorists. Officer Johnny Brooks has vowed to take serious precautions to prevent the repetition of such attacks." The news reader repeated the exact sentence for a hundred times, which annoyed Leanne to the very core. She switched it off and groaned in frustration. Out of all the men in the world, she was married to this 'guy' on TV, simply known as Victor Jones. He was arrested for the murder of his grandparents. After the day they parted, Victor was never the same; it was like he had a lingering feeling of a dangerous evil in his soul.

After all, it wasn't easy for her to balance her marital life with a suspected criminal. They were married, but Leanne hadn't ever heard about Victor's past. A past of his, before he met her. He was trying to hide something, possibly to shape his image in a good way among the others of the society. It changed his behaviour. He was left traumatized. Victor's past was the key to her solution.

The terrorist organization had demanded for a single man, and that was Victor himself. Great. Now she had the idea that her husband was a terrorist from Pakistan who had fallen in love with her on a mission. Right now, she was being hunted by the police. Someone else, had set the cops on her trail. Leanne was sure that someone connected to Victor had framed him. She didn't know why. Leanne needed answers.

As the final box of her pizza was over, Leanne opened up the shutter to the garage, and the sunlight hit her brown eyes. She jogged into the house beside her, and started the conversation with the two ididots tied to her kitchen stove, with a metal chain. "Who the hell is your damn master? Who the heck are you working for?"

One of the men responded, "The mistress is is coming, for the both of you. Fueled by anger, hatred and revenge, she won't stop till she tastes your flesh. The time has come, and she is out of the shadows. Run, with all your might, but for all I know, she is the hunter, and you are her prey."

"I asked you for information, not a damn warning." Leanne was exhausted. She casually poured a litre of kerosene on each of them, and cut the metal chains of their hands. They leapt up, and ran for quite a few seconds, till their hope faded away. Leanne lit up the cigarette in her mouth, and threw away the lighter, right on the guy's bald head. He flinched in pain.

They were on fire for a few seconds, with the loud screams of pain and agony. Meh. They deserved it. The fire died, and they were no more than a hunk of dead meat. It really didn't matter anyway. Leanne heard a wailing noise, which made her run back to the guest bedroom, slowly cradling the two year old toddler in her soft arms. She curled up next to the child herself. June. Since Victor had left her, Leanne was enduring the ache of sleepless nights. She wondered, if there would ever be a day when she could have a true family, to fill the empty void in her heart.

Nah. She didn't feel like sleeping now, either. Leanne grabbed a can of diet coke, along with another slice of mushroom-pizza in her right hand. She placed an archaic record on her gramophone, and the music quickly stirred up to the positive, high pitched voice of the lead singer. She did a distinct mix of salsa, flamenco, ballet and a waltz across the the floortiles of the room. Leanne had successfully chugged her seventh can of diet coke. She was drunk, and depressed. She continued dancing for another half an hour or so, till she succumbed to dizziness.

Leanne basked in the glory of her sadness, she rejoiced the music's vocals. The melody finally came to a halt, when the doorbell rang, repeatedly. The door creaked open, and there he was, smoking a cigar while entering the room. Slowly, Leanne backed away, towards a corner. "I'm here, darling. Don't fret. It's all gonna be over, now." She couldn't move, so she had to listen to the guy's demands.

"Give me the key, and I will spare you and her, alive. Or, we can have it the hard way," whispered Johnny, as he casually picked up two kitchen knives, placing one under Leanne's throat. On the other hand, Leanne was having serious doubts about her marriage. She suspected that this was Victor's doing. He would know better; sending a single cop to kill her was a completely disasterous idea.

As a part of her muscle memory and reflex action, Leanne kicked his balls, just before she plunged one of the kitchen knives into his right eye. She stripped Johnny of his belt, and his trousers came undone. She went further down the lane, by whipping the guy with an RCMP belt in one hand, and a skipping rope in the other. Leanne poured a pot of boiling water on his head, until he scampered away, leaving his belt and trousers behind.

"Man, the guy was weak as shit," muttered Leanne, who grabbed another slice of pizza. She picked up her I-Phone 13 and made a call. She needed to prepare. Leanne was going out. She sighed, while collapsing onto one of her leather-recliners. Her life was a total mess. From being a child without a mother to a failed marriage, Happiness was a rarely experienced feeling in her life. She hadn't met Victor in four years. She didn't know where he was, or what he was doing. Someone was targeting them both. A bigger source, who may have been interlinked to Victor's dangerous past, believed Leanne.

Leanne was going to fight back. Whoever was frightening them, the day would come. Four years of hiding was the biggest punishment she had ever experienced. Now she would make them run, cry, and hide. She would make them beg for mercy. She didn't want Victor. She wanted peace. Leanne only had a single clue to Victor's past. The name. Fiona Rodriguez. She needed to find her, to retrieve the answers she desired.

She closed her eyes, trying to imagine the day when she could live her life, as just an ordinary mother.

VI

The Faith Within

"What kind of a guy are you, Victor Jones? Cute, smart, stylish, respectful; isn't there anything bad about you?" Victor responded, "You are", as he wrapped his arms around Leanne's neck. Her mind had been dwelling on the past, ever since they had parted.

The picture, was taken in a retro style, with Victor and Leanne hanging from a tree, upside down, oblivious to the very horror that would have unfolded. The visit to Victor's apartment hadn't rekindled their relationship, but it implemented a strong sense of nostalgia in Leanne's mental health. After all, they had gotten married, because they could understand each other, their moods, problems and behaviours. Although economically different, the two of them had grown up in similar atmospheres, and the only comfort they found was within each other.

She had gotten to know a great deal about Victor's grandparents. Gregor Jones, however, was an indirect red flag to their marriage. To this day, Leanne thoroughly remembered the words of Gregor.

"This is a vault, which I have built using the money of your father's illegal operations. We cannot hand it over to the government, as I fear they will put the both of you behind bars. It will come in handy, for the both of you and the future generations. Use it wisely."

Saying so, he handed a key to Leanne, "The only way to open the vault requires this key, and Victor's signature."

Leanne fell down to her knees, helplessly. She grabbed a packet of meth from her backpack, inhaling it. She wasn't a drug addict, but she really needed something other than Coke to calm her down, something more effective. Her eyes were blurry, and she really didn't feel like moving. Her physicality was highly disabled by the drug.

She tried to reminisce the time when all hell broke loose. When things went awry. The very day a couple lost trust, love, and all means of communication with each other. That one moment between them, had caused her numerous sleepless nights.

*

It was a peaceful morning, a time when life was nothing short of exhilarating. Leanne was busy, spending time with June, watering the plants in their 'quite-large' garden. Leanne had married Victor, despite the fact he was the son of a criminal.

Leanne hadn't experienced a horrible childhood. She was raised in an orphanage, supported by a trust fund organization. She was financially set, had a talent at socializing, but she and Victor were searching for a common element. Having a family of their own.

Victor, who was busy at work, felt relieved. He now had someone, to truly look after and take care of him. With the burden of a nasty death away from his shoulders, he looked towards a brighter future.

Everyday, Victor would set off to work, while Leanne had a busy time, managing the household, and simaltaneously teaching karate in the zen garden in the backyard.

However, there was the essence of magic between them; they could make any situation work.

*

Victor entered the house, quivering. He bolted the doors, ran towards the windows, and drew the curtains. It was 10:30 PM.

"Leanne!"

She rushed down the stairs, with a worried feeling.

"What the hell happened to you?"

Victor looked frightened, as if he had seen the devil. Leanne could remember his fear-soaked expression to this day, and it wouldn't stop giving her nightmares.

"Leanne. Listen to me. We're not safe here. Pack your clothes. Now!"

"But why-"

"I said now!"

His voice sounded harsh, and hoarse, and Leanne felt vulnerable. Suddenly, Victor wasn't the type of peace-loving guy who loved the tranquility of nature.

She was trembling, with fear, half curious and half worried about the situation Victor was in, covered in sweat, wearing a threatening face. Leanne slowly walked up the stairs, and stopped. She was planning to make an announcement, but the situation hadn't demanded the unexpected news.

Victor collapsed onto the bed, after a long, hot shower. Throughout the night, he kept shivering, mumbling random hymns that madee no sense. However, Leanne could sense that he was deeply troubled.

*

That was the one significant memory that remained fresh, in Leanne's mind. The days used to pass, and Victor was slowly transitioning into a cold-blooded introvert. He would come home late, sweating, and frightened. There was something which endangered Victor, but he was just too afraid to let it out. There were days, times when he wrecked the house, in comeplete anger, while Leanne would just watch in horror. Time went by, and the relationship between the newly married couple was diminishing. Victor was mental, and Leanne pretended to push it away.

It was the second of July, 2020. A quiet dinner between Leanne and Victor, was in motion.

"Tell me. What the frick is going on? What the hell is happening? I don't know, Victor. Maybe you can tell me. Over the past few weeks, you've been acting like a complete animal, breaking plates and destroying the house? Goddamnit, tell me! I'm your wife!"

Victor stared at his vegetable salad in silence.

Leanne was cross.

Victor threw the plate at the window, scowling at Leanne. He stormed up to his room, and shut the door with a bang, as Leanne watched in tears and despair. Throughout the night, Victor heard noises from the kitchen, and regretted the fact that he had been so cruel to his very own wife. But he had no choice. He was going to deliberately distance himself from her.

It was an early morning, Victor had recieved a ton of missed calls frm the same exact number. He woke up, and headed down to make breakfast for himself, but there was no sign of Leanne, or her clothes. Instead, she had left a note, for him.

Dear Victor,

You see, life hasn't been so kind to me, ever since I was born. Growing up, without a family, in the shadow of an NGO hasn't benefited me as much. To this day, I continue my search for true happiness.

You have filled the empty void in my heart, at least, temporarily. But now, it seems like my happiness, is limited. I do not know, what's going on with you, and it seems that the pleasures of life have now corrupted your mind.

I know, that you won't break, and somehing is troubling you, but if it means that you're too good for your wife, Then I guess you're just as fickle minded.

I, am pregnent, and as every woman would like to have it, to celebrate the news. I, have realized the hard way, that I'm just not meant to be happy.

I'm leaving you, Victor. Hopefully, one day, all that arrogance and aggression of yours, will shed off.

Yours truly,

Leanne Smith.

As Victor reached the end of the letter, he grinned, in happiness, and agony. Leanne had left him for good, but now, she was safe. Unbeknownst to her, Victor was facing a big threat; a threat which would mean the end of the couple. As Victor fell down to his knees, wailing loudly, the doorbell rang.

Victor noticed several men, surrounding his house, all armed. The door was broken open, and in entered a bald man wearing a suit.

"Who the hell are you guys?"

The baldie stared at Victor, with a twisted eyebrow, and started to write a few notes on his sheet.

"Victor Jones, I'm going to need you to cooperate with me, for a second."

"Why?"

"Boys, cuff him."

The guards behind him handcuffed Victor.

"You, Victor Jones, are being arrested, due to domestic assault on your wife, Leanne Smith."

*

Victor was handcuffed, and was now being led to an asylum, after signing forged papers, which supposedly indicated that he was a patient with psychological issues. Sure, he was diagnosed with schizophrenia, but that didn't leave the cops to say that he was outright mental.

Fortunately, Victor had pulled off exactly what he had hoped to do. Leanne was away, and Victor in jail. She had sent him to an asylum in Canada, but Victor was satisfied, nevertheless.

He didn't care about living happily, not anymore. He just wanted Leanne to be safe, no matter whatever happened to him, Victor's mistake, had finally come back, to haunt him. Being in the lockup, wasn't any different, but now, it seemed like a matter of life and death.

The guard who was responsible for Victor's cell called out-

"A visitor for Victor Jones."

He hoped it would be Leanne, trying to apologize for the mistake she had done. He raced towards the conjugal visit area, where a familiar face, stood outside the glass window, waiting for him. Fiona.

She spoke through the phone, "Victor Jones, look where you are, right now. Your wife, has absconded, and you, a coward, are taking refuge in the damn jail."

"What do you want?"

"I want, to watch you die, Victor. The time has finally come. You, can no longer escape, and your death, is inevitable. This, is your last warning, Victor. Give me the documents, and you cann walk away, scot free."

"No."

"Very well, I guess, I have to do this the hard way. Look around, Victor. Everyone, you see, are my men. Within just a snap of my finger, you, will disintegrate. They will tear you to shreds, and you will bleed more. I have caused the separation between you two, and I'm the one who will kill you, and your wretched family."

As Victor watched a grinning Fiona walk away, he realized that she wasn't going to stop her ceaseless hunt for money, anytime soon, It was sheer, violent madness. It was now, the dawn of a new era, in Victor's life, and the time had finally come. It was clear, that Fiona had once again wrecked havoc, in his life. Victor had to fight, in order to live another day. Leanne was right. Life hadn't been so kind, to the two of them. As he went back to his jail cell, Victor realized that it would take a long time to set things right, once and for all.

VII

The Sketch

The 4 partners were standing in the 'Rosewood Garden' , to the front of 'Hibiscus House.' Technically, they weren't breaking into a house, but a full blown mansion, which was built by Terry Jones, after a long period of tax-evading crimes. They were waiting for an important guest. A guest who had led them to their billion-dollar fortune. They caused havoc in the garden, demolishing the entrence to the mansion's interior with a dozen of dynamite sticks. Everything they did was under the legal pretext of an income-tax raid.

Eight wasrooms, twenty-one bedrooms, and a living room which was the size of four guesthouses wasn't even a millionth of what the moolah hidden could buy. The house had polished and heated floors, a gigantic television, a private home theatre, and seventeen servants who one could spend time with if he/she didn't have any friends. However, what intrigued the four of them was the murky old basement, which was their one goal.

Next to the master bedroom, a huge, shiny padlock was spotted, which led to the basement. Johnny didn't have a key, considering which, he picked the lock. At the end of the deep, narrow, spiral staircase, was a big, metal room with a vault occupying half the given space. It was accurately the size of ten adult elephants, built with steel and diamond.

Ken walked over to the vault, slowly caressing its surface.

"Look, there it is. The Victorian Vault. It was built with the very metals, unearthed during the Victorian era." Johnny deduced, "Made of diamond, steel, copper, and a mixture of other alloys, just imagine. The very cost of making this took a large, large amount. This vault is our billion dollar lottery ticket!"

Grace smiled, "We can steal the money, if it were not contained in this vault. We need two specific items that can activate the technological mechanism of this vault. If we try to manually open or destroy it, the vault will be highly subjected to the risk of an self -destructing mechanism, which downs our chances to retrieve that moolah down to zero.

Ken continued, "Which is exactly why we need the involvement of Fiona here. She can easily evade the law with our help, so that the law does not gain suspicion of a corrupted department trying to aid a criminal. She does the job of threatening Victor, as he hold one of the crucial items, which is, a signature. It cannot be forged as Victor has never used it till this day. Leanne, who holds the key to the vault, is our target. Fiona is not familiar with the involvement of Leanne, which is why we have sent you, Johnny, to retrieve the key. But you were just too weak."

The gang walked up towards the surface of the mansion.

They informed the officials, stating that nothing was found in Victor's residence. Grace pulled out four strips of documented paper. Flight tickets to Mexico.

*

After what seemed like an eternity, the squad boarded their respective cabs, which all led to different parts of Mexico city. Using untraceable cell phones, they contacted different people, who were all interlinked to the same person.

John Kumar was given a scooter to ride, to the outskirts of Mexico City, an abandoned flour mill, where many sewage openings were present. The four of them were now at the very exact opening. They climbed down, using a termite infested ladder, and crawled through the big-but-not-too-big pipes, which finally led to a big, underground hideout, which was probably bigger than Victor's heavenly abode.

They slowly took their seats in the room next to where Fiona was standing; she was commanding many groups of criminals and corrupt officials, each assigned with a specific crime to commit.

After a while, Fiona, with blood stained hands, walked in and pulled a chair, starting a conversation with John Kumar.

"Is the job done?"

"Yes. Victor's frightened out of his very wits, the law is oblivious to the wrongdoing, but there is one final problem which you do need to take care of."

"And what is that, Kumar?"

"Leanne Smith. She is Victor's wife, who has the key to the vault. Once we have our hands on it, the ball will be in our court."

"Very well, then. I will see to it, that Leanne, will get my condolences."

Saying so, Fiona handed a large chainsaw to John Kumar, and left the room.

Part Two

Retribution

VIII

A Dry Secret, A Past In Hell

There he lay, on the blanket, over the grass, in the forest behind the campus, holding hands with the devil in disguise, aka Fiona Rodriguez. Her very presence, caused Victor to feel exhilerated. They stared at each other, wondering how they could be so alike, physically and mentally. The same ocean-blue eyes, chocolate-brown hair, and the quiet, calm personality. They were made for each other. Victor was gullible, and so he fell into Fiona's trap.

"Look, Fiona, the sky. You see those stars? The big one, is me. The other one, is you. The tiny one in the middle, is what I hope to have, as an extension of our family. Our child."

Fiona smirked, "Looking at the sky reminds me of something else."

"And what is that?"

"The sky, so dark, so gloomy. This would be a perfect spot to mercilessly slaughter a hundred Nazis using a bucher knife."

"Damn."

It was 2016, February 3rd. Victor was a student of engineering, who had just begun to appreciate the optimism in life, after a dull childhood. Jin Maple's Institution Of Excellence had given him a new lease of life. His curriculum was simple, he enjoyed the tranquility of being in nature, and most importantly, Victor had found himself the one he was looking for. His only possible source of happiness. Fiona was an ambitious girl with quite a few limitations. She had a wicked sense of humor, was indisciplined, and was a huge fan of Ryan Reynolds.

Victor was an Introvert. There wasn't any doubt about it. He liked being alone, studying in the library, or inhaling the fresh perfume of dandelions with Fiona, while listening to a Taylor Swift album. Life was perfect in college. In the holidays, he would head back home, spending time with his grandparents, and wouldn't miss the chance to create a memory or two with them.

Fiona was a good partner. His relationship with her was smoother than the roads in Singapore. However, Victor's suspicion soon evolved into a problem. He didn't know a goddamn word about her family, or even her social background. What the hell was even her last name? All that Victor knew was the one-dimentional side of Fiona, a girl who was hiding a lot of secrets from the one she was plotting on.

It so happened, that one fine day, It was Victor's birthday.

"Fiona, what the frick happened? You look dirty, and there's goddamn blood on your hands!"

"Victor, Chill out. It was just a frickin tramp. Look at me now, I'm alive. Damn, that guy had a hundred dollars on him."

"What the heck? You just killed a pauper for money? I can't believe you!"

"You're making a big deal of this frickin bullshit. The guy was just a damned beggar. He has no life, family or friends. So who the hell cares?

"Fiona, Imma have to call the cops on you."

"Shut it, you goddamn shithole. Look, I know, you haven't asked me anything about my family, or who I really am. I guess it's time to show you."

"What the heck do you mean? Fiona, I'm being serious, If you're a criminal..."

"Follow me, Vic. I'll explain everything."

Fiona, who was covered in sweat and blood, led Victor down a narrow alleyway, which consisted of numerous old and abandoned houses. They finally came to a large sewer opening, where they climed down the metal ladder, giving way to a large space underground, an abandoned subway station. Fiona led him to a huge chamber, with hundreds of people.

Victor, his eyes wide with disbelief, stared at Fiona as she proudly led him through the dimly lit, abandoned subway station. The air was thick with the stench of sweat and gasoline, as her ruthless biker gang roared around them. He couldn't believe this was the same woman he loved.

"Vic, you gotta understand, this is my world now," Fiona said defiantly, her voice tinged with a hint of pride. "I built this empire from nothing, and I won't let anyone take it away from me. Money talks, and we're fluent in it."

As Victor tried to process the shocking revelation, he found himself questioning the woman he thought he knew. The crime-laced air around them seemed to symbolize the crumbling of their relationship, leaving behind a cold, hard reality that would haunt him for a long time to come.

"Join me, Vic. We can rule the world. This isn't you. After all, your father was my very role model."

Victor, wide-eyed and trembling, stared at the ruthless gang led by the fierce Fiona, who smirked as she reveled in her power. "What the hell, Fiona? You've turned into one of these monsters?!" He couldn't believe the woman he loved was responsible for such chaos and violence. Fiona, unfazed by his reaction, responded with a venomous grin, " You thought I was just some sweet, innocent girl? This is who I am, and I won't change for you or anyone else. Happy birthday, dear Victor. This is my world now, and if you can't accept it, maybe you don't belong here." The tension between them escalated, and as they argued, a sudden, unexpected explosion rocked the abandoned subway station, plunging them both into a haze of smoke and chaos, their future uncertain amidst the chaos they had created. Fiona wasn't who she really claimed to be, after all.

Two weeks later, Victor recovered, from a major injury he had gone through. A part of him wanted to run over to the nearest police station and snitch about the wrongdoings of Fiona, but he also loved her to an extent that he would commit suicide for her sake.

Time passed. Days turned into weeks, and weeks turned into months. Victor wondered where Fiona was. He did care about her.

Victor's heart raced with worry as he approached his teacher, Mrs. Jenkins, after class. "Excuse me, Mrs. Jenkins," he began, trying to keep his voice steady. "I have a question about Fiona Rodriguez. She's my friend, and I haven't seen her in days. Do you know where she might be?" Mrs. Jenkins furrowed her brow, studying Victor's face with concern.

"I'm sorry, Victor, but there's no student by that name enrolled at our school. Are you sure she's a student here?"

Victor's world seemed to spin as the words registered in his mind. "What do you mean she's not here? Fiona and I have been together for months. She always talked about her classes and friends here." His voice quivered with disbelief.

Mrs. Jenkins placed a gentle hand on his shoulder, her eyes filled with sympathy. "I'm truly sorry, Victor. But I assure you, there is no Fiona Rodriguez at our school. Is there anyone else who might know where she is?" Victor stood there in shock, the weight of uncertainty crushing down on him. Where was Fiona, and why was there no trace of her in the place she was supposed to be?

Victor raced down to the abandoned subway, where the sewer pipeline was now filled to the brim with cement. Something was wrong, Fiona was missing, and the underground chamber of criminals he had seen yesterday, was filled up like it never existed.

He went back to his dormitory, carrying an uneasy feeling. He sat in front of the bonfire, contemplating about Fiona's whereabouts. As the days passed, he was slowly feeling vulnerable. Victor stared into the soul of the deep, blazing hot fire. He had to take a desicion.

He saw a blurry figure, entering the campus grounds. It was Fiona.

He brought out the knife, and it all went down in a second. The cutlery, landed the killing blow.

*

The rain was perfectly in sync with Victor's emotion. Depressing, Blood poured down Fiona's body, just like Victor's tears. He had murdered his lover, and now he was mourning her very death. However mentally unstable he was, Fiona was the real psycho in this situation. Death never was a beautiful sight.

He dragged her, across the boundries of the dormitory, Leaving her dead, in the midst of a forest.

Days passed, and there was no sign of a dead carcass in the woods. Victor feared a day, when his past would come back to haunt him. Was Fiona still alive, and would she just be searching for him?

IX

Scars Of Nostalgia

Victor, was now in his final year of engineering, he had forcefully moved to another state, with the memory of Fiona's death fresh in his mind.

He now stayed at a hotel, he accepted no visitors, being a lonely man; the only company he had was the room service that entered his space occasionally. Now, he had logged out of all social media accounts, trying to be protective about his family.

He would take extreme precautions, just to go outside. After a few months of cautious living, Victor had earned his degree, beginning to feel less vulnerable against the coming danger.

*

The Dinner

- As of today, Room service is no longer exercised by the management. Residents will have to manually serve themselves.

· The management is also hosting a party in the function hall at 7:00 PM in the evening. A list of guidelines must be followed-

1. The residents are not permitted to enter the hall without formal clothing.
2. Outsiders are strictly not permitted to enter.
3. One man, who will identify as Victor Jones, shall not be treated with any disrespect.

Regards,
Jack

Nope. Victor wasn't an actor or politician to recieve respect and Z- Level Security from everybody around him. He guessed that something was queer, but decided to go anyway.

At six-thirty in the evening, Victor was dressed, wearing a maroon tuxedo, his face powdered with makeup, and his hair pointed sidewards due to the excess gel. One could have called his appearance a 'Dress Of Seeking Attention.' He headed downwards to the dinner hall, where the place was packed with hundreds of people and a variety of cusines for the guests to try. There were multiple air conditioners attatched to the roof, with heated floors below. A huge jaccuzzi was at a corner of the space, filled with topless men.

Victor had done his research. The owner was a well-known investment banker who founded a group of hotels such as this one. They were economically thriving, but were also a big target in the eyes of a criminal. He realized that he had made the biggest mistake of his life. The third guideline from the note which was stuck to his door, was a sign of the trap.

*

It was dark; the mains were deprived of electricity.

The highly disturbing noises of multiple machine guns echoed throughout the hall. It was a horrible experience for Victor to witness. The white walls, were now stained with a vibrant splash of red all around. There she was, a machete in one hand, and the limb of a person in another. Victor couldn't believe his eyes. Fiona. The Devil's reincarnation. Victor guessed that she was bloodthirsty for revenge.

She held Victor's surprisingly delicate hands, lifting them up, and down, syncing to the music playing on the vinyl record, slowly dancing to the rhythm of a 1980's ballet playlist. They stared into each other's eyes, moving their balance from one foot to another, giving Victor the taste of nostalgia. As the music ended on a high note, Fiona ruffled his hair.

"Well, look what we have here. A healthy mortal, all limbs intact, a clean face, and a large packet of blood. My dear companion, Victor Jones," said she, holding the machete right under Victor's throat.

Victor was terrified as hell, however, he showed no sign of his weakness. "I'm goddamn innocent. You're the one who brought up a large empire. You're the one that tried to steal from the poor."

"Innocent? You? You're frickin innocent? You stabbed me! Again and again, till I had a sure shot at dying. You dumped me in the forest. I was still alive, bleeding, left alone, like a decomposed body. All these months, and you don't show a single sign of remorse. "

"No. You can't do this. You loved me. You don't have the heart to kill me!"

"Me? You? Shut your goddamn hole, Victor. I love money, and I live, for money. You see, the underworld maintains strong relations. When I heard of Terry Jones' death, I felt fortunate. I learnt about you, a complete wastrel, holding on to the billions your father had, using it for nothing. Now, I had an idea. Being a perfectionist in money matters, I hatched up a plan, to trap you in my web."

Fiona brought the torch closer to Victor's face, "But you were just too afraid, poor, gullible Victor. Beware, Victor Jones, I will not forget the deed that has been done. You have had your fun. And now, it is my turn. I will soon return, and there will be no forgiveness. I will show you hell."

Fiona walked away, pointing her finger at a corpse, as a traumatized Victor realized, that his death was near.

X

Justice Is Blind, But John Kumar Isn't

Damn. Victor was in the court of law, a place which he hadn't expected to be in after his highly detailed confession. He had hoped that the defence minister would have a tinge of sympathy on hearing his story, but Victor realized that once again, he had fallen prey to his weak conscience.

It was nine-thirty in the morning, and Victor was busily grumbling about Ken's betrayal towards him. Following the first session, Victor had a few more dngerous interactions with Grace, AKA, the mentally deranged psychiatrist, who was seemingly obsessed by the very mentality of criminals, in spite of Victor failing to be one.

In his last session, his face was pale, for he was subjected to a distinct method of torture, which included him being thrown into a bathtub of leeches, which wasn't exactly a beautiful sight.

Now, he was taken to the court of law, where his future was to be decided. Victor wanted to live in a village, with an overdose of peace and love, where he could imagine the time before he had gotten into this one heck of a mess.

His imagination was disrupted by the two constables beside him, watching and frequently chatting about the same soap opera, while drinking a hot glass of black coffee.

The court finally came to the matter of Victor's case, which was obviously a serious one. Victor gazed at the judge, Justice Kumar, who was busy chatting on his phone.

"The court will now dwell upon the hearing of Victor Jones and Fiona Rodriguez. As the latter has been absent, the focus will now shift upon Victor and his perspective of the murder."

The prosecutor stood up, banging a pile of case files onto the bench.

"Your honor, this man isn't the type of an 'Ordinary Joe' he claims to be. Every human, consists of two visible shades, good and bad. But here, this man's mind is deprived of its positivity. Victor Jones, the defendant, has committed a crime. He has been arrested for the murder of his grandparents, Gregor and Genilia Jones. There are also documented reports of his behaviour during his time spent at 'The Ruffians Mansion'. " The prosecutor handed over a file from his collection, to the judge.

The defending lawyer was playing 'Candy Crush' , rather than being engrossed in the matter of Victor's pride, integrity and innocence.

"That's not all. Victor has also had a past connection with dangerous criminal Fiona Rodriguez, who was presumed to be his lover. With your permission, may I present a couple of witnesses who can describe Victor's atrocities in detail?"

Justice Kumar had this in the bag. Everything was going well, as planned.

"Yes, you may."

A tall, unshaven guy who had messy hair and tattered clothes, walked onto the witness' platform. He was obviously a beggar, who had probably been bribed by an officer to utter a false statement.

He surprisingly pulled out an I-Phone from his pocket, handing it over to Justice Kumar as a part of the evidence, along with a chainsaw, sealed in a huge transparent bag.

"Victor is a thief. This man was caught on video, breaking into the house of an elderly lady, wearing a mask, and trying to threaten her with a chainsaw. He then left the house, after murdering her. Since that day, the cops are still trying to recover the complete limbs of the woman. There is evidence against him. His fingerprints have been found on the chainsaw, which he surprisingly left at the crime scene. His hair samples have also matched with the ones found on the crime scene."

Victor kept mum. He knew that he couldn't prove his innocence this time. He guessed that Fiona had bought off all the important officials of the law, who were dealing with Victor's case, which would have also included Grace.

The prosecutor continued, "This video shown how his behaviour can be. May I also remind you that he has been a patient of an asylum for a couple of years? I would like to call upon my second witness."

Now, two muslims were the ones against him. Victor hadn't violently provoked anyone in the clear past.

"These brothers are the prisoners who were locked up in the cell opposite to Victor. They say that he howls every night, screaming repeatedly, till the guards were called to take control. He was even subjected to severe punishment for allegedly religiously insulting the two of them for the sake of entertainment. This incident proves that he is a psychop uath whose only purpose is to be contained for psychological purposes."

Victor was mad. He couldn't have beaten up anybody, and he was severly tortured only for the sake of psychological purposes. If Victor was right, Fiona had twisted the entire statement of the case. It seemed like every person he met, hated him.

Amidst all this, The constable behind him was listening to a cooking podcast through his earphones.

Finally, the defence lawyer spoke up, for which seemed like the first time Victor felt relieved.

"Your honor, I would like to make a suggestion. This video of Victor breaking and entering should be sent to the techies, as I fear a case of 'Deepfake' material has been used against Victor. His DNA might have also been deliberately placed on the spot, which is why I would like to suggest a method of deeper investigation. Also, I would like to request the court to temporarily shift Victor to his mansion in London, where he can be kept on house arrest until further evidence is in hand. The psychiatrist, Dr Grace Collins, should be reprimanded for her violent treatment of criminals, which involves the use of other prisoners."

The prosecutor intervened, "Objection, your honor. Let us take consideration of the fact that Victor Jones was the only one who was demanded for when a terrorist attack had occured recently. Hence, he is still a crucial suspect. Letting this man go would bring danger and disgrace to the entire country."

For a short while, the court was in silence, trying to process all the information that had been provided. Justice Kumar, who was flipping through the pages of the case file, immediately stood up.

"This case, is not to be finished within a single hearing. It has been classified as an issue to the entire department.

Investigation shall take place, Victor shall be kept on house arrest temporarily, and Dr Grace Collins will be reprimanded considering her interactions with Victor. I am ordering the local police to bring me additional information about the accused. The court is adjourned for lunch."

Victor wasn't happy about the judgement, even though he was going back to his house in London. He had a bad feeling about Justice Kumar's actions. He strolled towards Victor.

The lawyer left the two of them alone, and they spent the next few minutes looking at each other, seriously.

Justice Kumar grinned, "You cannot escape. We've been tracking you, for the past few years. You will be hunted, like a deer on the run. It's too late. She has returned, and now, bloodshed is nothing but imminent. Your desicion, on that very, fateful day, has now become your death warrant. Fiona Rodriguez. Your killer. She was born, to kill, torture and frighten you. She is the bane you have always underestimated. Farewell, dear friend, Victor Jones. You will die in the hands of the destined one. And I, shall attend your funeral in utmost happiness."

Saying so, Justice Kumar left the courtroom, smiling to himself, pleased at his attempt to frighten Victor using the details of the guy's own past.

Victor collapsed onto the floor. He leaned against the hard surface of the witness' platform, repeatedly banging his knuckles onto the wooden floor, till his wrist bled. Justice Kumar's words echoed in Victor's mind. He had realized that his death was now inevitable. All he could do, was scream in frustration, while etching the name of his wife. Before his untimely death, Victor had one last wish to fulfil. Leanne Smith. It was a name, that couldn't be erased from his mind.

XI

The Painful Truth

Victor was tied up; he was being threatened at his own residence by the people whom he hated the most. It was irony. His vision was blurry; he never was much of a television addict. He was the kind of guy who enjoyed and thoroughly experienced the bliss of peaceful atmospheres. He was a 29 year old, who was the son of an egoistic mobster. His very lineage had brought his life to the very brink of being extinct.

Grace was watching Netflix, while the others had gone out to possibly scheme on the topic of ruining people's lives for money. He closed his eyes, trying to relive the moment in which he had first met Leanne. To this day, he still couldn't decipher why he ever thought of settling down or starting a family with her. He was the son of a hardened criminal, not an accountant who loved his offspring. Following his encounter with Fiona, Victor had completely thrown out his emotions into a box, burying it deep, in the ground.

Victor remembered the guy who was responsible for his fate. His dad. Terry Jones. His life before he met Leanne. A life of complete negligence.

*

Victor was born in the 90s, where the crime rate was surging higher than the stock market in London. Terry Jones was a failed graduate who was a bad student, a bad husband, a bad father, and a bad child. His focus was ultimately directed towards money, and nothing else. Since his birth, Victor barely had someone to interact with, making him an introvert.

Terry Jones, who had failed to clear his degree in his thirties after repeated attempts, turned to a life of crime, in order to sustain his family. He soon found a way to earn more money than required, without getting apprehended by the law. His risky profession for the sake of sustainability slowly became into a greedy habit, which eventually broke his family.

His mother had passed away, before Victor could even learn how to speak. He only had three people, to confide in, during his upbringing. He was slowly subjected to the pain of lonliness. Victor's father didn't care about the family. Sur Victor had all the riches that a normal kid wouldn't have, but he desperately needed someone to fill in the empty space in his heart. It was like being an orphan. Victor only had his grandparents for mental support.

Things became worse when Terry passed away, succumbing to his injuries from a gang war. Gregor and Genilia Jones, Victor's grandparents, shared the same mentality as him. They were his real parents. Around them and their lifestyle, Victor could finally sense a feeling of reat joy; his mental nealth was more stable, and everyday seemed to burn the cobwebs in his mind, However, he felt a sensation of lonliness, somewhere, in his heart.

Tery had collected huge amounts of black money through illegal operations, before his death. Fearing the lockup, Victor and Gregor used fake documents and created false backstories to create a reason for the huge stash of money they were storing in the mansion in London.

Before he knew it, Victor had turned 23, promising himself that he would no longer evade the law, having to live a normal and a peaceful life.

After his graduation and a few months of interrogation due to Fiona's involvement, Victor was broken. He had gotten a job and was now free from the cops. However, what Fiona said to him on that fateful day roared in his mind, affecting his mental health drastically. He avoided as many as he could. He wouldn't open up to anybody about what happened on that day. Victor had been relocated, following his traumatic experience in the hotel massacre. The law had promised to provide security, as long as he as proved innocent of being Fiona's aide. Having proven himself as an innocent, through the basis of unclear evidence, Victor had been deported to Canada, for a short while.

*

The forest. The one place where Victor found solace in. The chirping birds and the whistling winds, reminding him of the time when life wasn't a nightmare. He lay against the bark of the tree, closed his eyes, trying to experience the sensation of true peace.

"Feels good, doesn't it? The sounds of nature. Being away from the nature, taking a deep breath, and trying to reminisce all that you have loved in your life."

Victor's head spun around.

There she was, dressed in ripped jeans and a leather jacket, with her back rested against a tree, just like Victor. He was undoubtedly lost in her brown eyes.

"Nice to meet you. The name's Victor."

"Oh. You're the guy who's dad died a decade ago in a gang war. Damn."

Victor found it quite insulting for someone to address him like that, but he kept quiet, wondering if he could build a stronger relation with her.

"By the way, my name's Leanne, and I'm currently jobless. Do you come around here often?"

"Yeah."

"Cool."

As they talked, Victor could feel a sense of similarity between the two of them. Knowingly or unknowingly, they had hit it off. Victor had found nature's perfect gift. She was going to help Victor forget. Forget everything he had ever gone through. Victor could tell that even Leanne felt an emotional connection between them.

Victor didn't know much about her life. His everyday routine, however, was now brighter than he had expected. Everyday, he would head off to work, and after an exhausting period of boredom, he would arrive at the same spot at the forest, in the evening, where he had a conversation with Leanne.

Months passed, and Victor had started to focus only on the good things in life, which was his supposed number one philosophy. He was now closer to Leanne, the both of them, sitting next to each other, closing their eyes, and living in the moment. Neither of them tried to propose. They knew what was happening, and they were ready to embrace the arriving future.

They slowly became emotionally closer, and one day, Victor felt that it was finally time to break out.

*

It was a sunday. Victor spent the last fourteen hours, trying to muster up the courage. He had a bouquet of roses in hand, wearing a tuxedo. He drove towards the forest, starting from the steep hill above the clinic. Victor strolled, slowly towards the back of the tree, sitting down, with his head rested against it, as usual.

"You're early."

"Thanks for the bunch of roses."

Victor rolled onto her lap, beginning his monologue.

"You know, I feel, special. Look, I haven't exactly had a perfect life, until I met you. The moment I saw you, that day, leaning against the trees, I realized that there was a spark that ignited, between the two of us. I just feel that you, should be with me. We share a common mindset, and although we don't know much about each other, I'm coming of age, and I'd like to try something new for once."

"What are you implying, dumbass?"

"I say, that I want to start a new journey. A journey with you."

Leanne ruffled his hair, "I'm stubborn."

"I'll put up with you."

"I'm a psycho."

Yeah, and I'm a therapist."

"I got no family."

" I'll be there."

Leanne gave in, as she hugged Victor, in a tight embrace, as fireworks lit up the sky, a perfect moment, to remember and reminisce.

It was the beginning of a new life. Somehow, Victor's perseverance had finally paid off, as for the first time in his life, a wonderful future lay ahead, as Victor had a smile on his face, in spite of him currently being threatened and tied to a chair.

*

He opened his eyes, and his grin faded, ad Victor's mind once again came back to the harsh reality. A black figure, was slowly walking towards him. The same devilish grin, lookalike features, gave him goosebumps. Victor was now face to face with the demon of his dreams.

"Well, Look who we have here, an orphan. An orphan who chooses peace over violence. Responsibilty over money. My darling, Victor Jones."

"What the frick do you want? If it's money, then I'll give you my signature. Leave me alone."

"Oh no, sweet, dear Victor has surrendered. I don't only want the money. I want to see the look of despair on your face."

"Fiona, I'm telling you, get your filthy hands off my family-"

"Shut up! You don't get to talk. You need to experience me. I wanna watch you burn, Victor, and not just physically. I want you to emotionally tear your heart out, when you watch your family collapse."

Fiona grinned, walking away, as she shut the doors and closed the windows to the mansion.

Victor, was now alone. He was half-heartedly hoping for his family's survival. Right now, his grandparents were dead, he was framed for multiple crimes, and he was tied up to a chair, with his nose and forehead bleeding. The almighty wouldn't have been this cruel on the others.

With his last bit of strength, he shut his eyes, praying, hoping that his untimely message, would reach its destination. He wanted to meet Leanne, for one last time. He wanted to sleep in her arms again. He wanted to live a peaceful life, with the one thing he wanted most. A family.

XII

Care

Things were going horribly wrong for Leanne. She hadn't heard from her husband in years, now gripped with the news of his deceased grandparents. She had broken into Victor's flat without definite permission from the cops. She stared at the broken pictures on the floor, and couldn't seem to apprehend the situation. However, the matter was straightforward. A person whom Victor might have had close relations with was now back to possibly harm him in any way. It affected Leanne mentally. The two of them were being hunted, but for what reason? Leanne was lost, looking for answers. The past three years of her life was nothing but a pain in the neck.

She headed back to her hotel room, where she collapsed onto the bed, thinking hard. Victor was missing. Sure, she had heard the news of him being thrown into an asylum, but something told her that the cops were a part of this dirty game, especially after a cop came to her residence, trying to assault her.

She had negligible options remaining, in her quest for peace. However, her desperation emulated her basic senses.

*

She was back, at the place where all hell would break loose, everyday. The strange alleyways of London, which was probably the one location where Victor's whereabouts could be extracted, for a price. The black market wasn't exactly a appropriate place to bring a newborn to. Leanne had to take the risks.

She strolled over to the dustbin where the cigarette butts had been disposed of. Leanne slid through a newly opened crack in the cement, where dozens of men stared at her, in surprise. She was now in a illegally renovated gigantic sewage tank.

"I wanna meet David."

A man dressed like a bartender responded. "He's currently occupied at the moment."

Leanne slid a wad of cash on the table.

"Right this way."

She walked past a shady beer parlour, filled with men and their questionable motives, along a room with people doing drugs. The baby strapped to her back recieved all the attention. The bartender opened a door, leading to a posh cabin, with an occupied leather chair at the centre.

The man looked up from his phone, seemingly interested. in Leanne. He was large, wearing a brown suit, had white hair, with brown eyes, and his face was wrinkled. The guy was a middle-aged criminal, who was the type of weirdo infatuated with stolen house utensils, which basically made him a drug-addict salesman.

"Ah, Leanne. You may sit. Come to sell the baby, perhaps?"

She clenched her fists.

"I need a piece of valuble information. Reason? It's complicated."

"Ah. For a price, that will do. What do you need, exactly?"

"Have you heard of this guy named Victor Jones?"

"Yeah. The guy who murdered his siblings, or whatever. My men scavenged his house for valuble material. He seemed to be a poor man."

"Have your men stumbled across a note, or a message, probably?"

"You see, Leanne, My men were paid to scavenge all the items from his house, and I let them keep everything they wanted, except for one, tiny, archaic, piece of paper. A note! Surprisingly, I have discovered, that he is your husband."

"Yeah, so, what's the price?"

David's voice was hoarse, "My financial gain has been amazing, surprisingly. A few days ago, I recieved a quite interesting offer from a customer named Fiona. A very intriguing person, she. As I was saying, Fiona offered me a million dollars, after getting to know the fact that you were my frequent customer, and that you bought drugs from me! Now, I've one simple task- Handing you over to Fiona."

"Try all you can, fatso, but I'm not a toy."

As David signaled the two bodyguards behind him, Leanne grabbed the gun on the table, pounding the trigger repeatedly till blood flowed freely from their chests. She tightened her grip on David's throat, pointing the gun in his gobhole.

"You want more?"

"Certainly."

She threw David out of the room, where the commotion spread all across the area. Several men got up from their seats, and Leanne guessed they were waiting for her arrival.

She was going to have a fun time. Leanne blocked June's ears with a pair of Headphones

She pulled out a dagger from her belt, "Get ready, boys."

Leanne was on a roll, and this bold night of hers' was turning oout to be a massacre. She sliced her way throughout the masculline army, covered in blood and sweat, literally. She wasn't any better than a criminal, but she was a karate instructor.

*

At the end of her unexpected cardio workout, Leanne had five-hundred calories burnt, along with completely blood soaked apparel, and a wine bottle piercing through every single body. David however, had crawled towards a corner while Leanne was busy beating the shit out of the gang.

"You were talking about a note?"

"I'll give it to you, absolutely free of cost!"

David ran to his 'Chest Of Valuable Items' and rummaged through the pile for about two minutes, which felt awkward.

"Yep. Here it is."

Leanne snatched the folded paper from David, taking a look at the message written for her.

Dear Leanne,

I know that you still possibly fear me. I have become endangered, and so might you. No harm shall befall me, as my memories are the only thing I need.

I'm afraid that my time on earth is diminishing, slowly. This is the price I have to pay. Run, run away, as far as you can.

I'm the one responsible for what's been happening to you. I've decided, to end it myself. I just wanna say, I'm sorry.

A few years ago, when I met you, it was certain that I would have someone, to look out for me. The very family that I had built with you, is now being demolished due to my actions.

This is my fault. Leanne, whatever you do, be careful. You might have heard of her. Fiona Rodriguez. My former girlfriend.

She is the cause of what has happened, so far. She has a thirst for money, and she won't stop till she retrieves the valubles in the vault. She will hunt you down till her goal is achieved.

I forgive you. In my time at the asylum, The only thing that kept me company, were our memories. Fiona. She is the one that has caused our separation. I'm not a psycho. I'm just scared. As everyday passes, I'm struck with the possibility of your death.

I love you, Leanne. Be safe, You and the baby.

Yours Truly,

Victor Jones.

Leanne fell onto the floor, in shock. Victor was framed. He was trapped. Tortured. She could do nothing. June wailed, as the headphones from her ears fell out. Knowingly or unknowingly, Leanne had sent Victor to hell. As tears made their way out of her eyes and onto the floor, Anyone could have guessed; Leanne still had feelings for Victor, and she wouldn't let them go.

Life was hard, and now she had nobody. It was all her fault. Only if she could change it.

Leanne wiped her tears and smiled. She wasn't going to run as Victor advised. Leanne was going to Hibiscus House, where she guessed Victor would be.

*

Leanne left, sealing the crack in the cement floor, which closed the opening to a space full of corpses, including David, who was hanging from the ceiling fan. She put on her headphones and hummed to a Taylor Swift album.

As she checked out of her hotel room, Leanne realized that she was about to take the biggest risk of all time. She was going to the place where the danger resided, and she wasn't afraid. She would mercilessly slaughter Fiona, and finally settle the score, once and for all.

XIII

A Grand Finale

Victor was waiting. He was anxiously killing time, trying to count the exact number of sheep that appeared in his head, a minute ago. The house was pitch black; Fiona and the gang had shut all the curtains, tying Victor's mouth with an ice-cold cloth. He was desparately hoping that someone would free him from her clutches.

His arms were tied to the chains hanging from the roof, and he was exhausted. He tried to scream, but in vain.

*

Fiona was about two centimetres away from him, dumping multiple sacks of gunpowder around the house, and placing a stick of dynamite right before his very nose.

She sat in a wooden chair, and set her stopwatch to beep at an hour.

"Now Victor, I haven't gotten confirmation yet, but I'm pretty sure that all I need are two dozens of higly skilled men, for the job. Now, I'm gonna need you to hand over the signed documents in an hour, or, we can do this the hard way."

Fiona waited for a response, in the gap of Victor mumbling hymns and poems about Jesus.

"You gotta give me the documents, else, you can say bye-bye to your existance."

"Nah, go kill yourself."

Fiona smiled. "Very well then. People, we have exactly an hour to find these papers, before I lose control of my sympathetic personality."

The five of them rummaged around the house searching for the signed documents, their search coming to a bad end, when the doorbell rang.

"Don't open it."

The doorbell rang again.

There was utter silence.

The doorbell rang a third time.

Fiona clenched her fists. "Who the frick is it?"

As the doorbell rang one more time, Victor broke into an unusual, unexpected smile. He knew who it was, and now, death was certain for Fiona.

The wooden door crumbled into pieces, and only a shadowy figure was seen, standing on the doorstep, with a dagger in hand, and a mind fueled by revenge.

Victor smiled. "She's a badass."

Leanne pounced onto Fiona, and the two of them began wrestling, pulling hair, shredding clothes and sustaining injuries.

Johnny and the others surrounded Leanne, waiting for a chance to eliminate her.

"You should be dead!"

"You, should have sent stronger men to kill me."

Fiona was miffed. She couldn't lose her one and only billion-dollar chance to a mere karate instructor.

She pulled a gun out, aiming the trigger at Leanne's forehead.

Fiona spoke in a hoarse, demeaning voice, "You better shut the hell up, Leanne. I've got your little husband in my grasp, and unless you wanna take a bullet through your sick forehead, be a darling, and give me the key."

"Meh. I'll take my chances."

The two grown women, who were now engaged in a brutal fistfight, rained punches on each other, left, right, and centre; Johnny and the rest of the gang were now in on the act. The situation was now getting worse; it was five against one.

She felt physical pain. She was being attacked from all sides, and her vision was blurry. She was dizzy, and even the drugs couldn't come to her rescue. She fell down, onto her knees, and even Victor's cries weren't enough to strengthen her.

*

Leanne heard voices, screaming. The voices of Victor, his grandparents, and herself. Would she be facing the same fate? To this day, a part of her thoroughly regretted what she had done to Victor, in the past. She was weak. Although a karate instructor, she had fallen flat, onto the floor, and she was probably dead. For the first time in her life, she had something worth fighting for, and she wasn't about to let it go that easily. She smiled, thinking of the happy memories she shared, with Victor. He was now tied to chains, left to die, in a house filled with gunpowder. She wasn't going to let that happen.

As Leanne tried to mentally prepare herself, the voices in her head started cheering her on, and now, she felt rejuvinated. Leanne, with difficulty, stood up, and grabbed her knife, stabbing a distracted Fiona in the throat.

As she grasped her neck, falling onto the floor, with blood flowing out of her like a stream, Leanne sat down, looking at Fiona, as the others watched in shock. She raised her hand, as a sign of despair and disgust, trying to question Leanne's motives, for one last time.

"You coward."

"You touch my family, you get the knife."

"No! Give me the documents, Give it to-"

As Fiona's movement came to stillness, The gang of four were in silence.

John Kumar, who was trembling with fear, went over to Leanne with folded palms, while the others began to free an unconscious Victor from his captivity.

"You'll have to agree to whatever I say, in the court of law, or else, the cops will find a dozen knives in each of your heads..." Leanne headed over to the master bedroom, along with a mystified June, who was busy watching the bloodshed from the kitchen.

She collapsed onto the bed, feeling the soft fabric of the pillow cushion her bleeding face. She had finally done it. In a few months, they would be free from the law, declared innocent, ready to start a new life, once again. Leanne looked up towards the celing, realizing that sadness and sorrow weren't the emotions that belonged in her life anymore. It was finally time, to break free from the hardships she had gone through.

*

There he was, standing on the cemented path, holding a bunch of flowers, standing in the very presence of a deceased Fiona Rodriguez. Sure, Victor's life had gone to the dogs, but it was she who still held a special place in Victor's journey.

Beside him, was an injured Leanne, who was discharged from the hospital, following an abdominal surgery. Victor placed his bouquet on the hard cemented roof of the gravestone, kneeling down, and muttered a few christian hymns. As Leanne watched on with a straight face, she couldn't help but feel a little sorry. Fiona may have been a bad person, but she knew that Victor believed in her.

Neither Victor nor the government had any information on Fiona. Nobody knew where she came from or what her ulterior motive was. Fiona could have become a better person. Nobody knew if she was forced into crime or was a descendant of a criminal. All the Victor hoped for, was for Fiona to change, for the greater good.

As Victor said goodbye to Fiona's grave, he placed an envelope in the bouquet, slowly walking away, holding hands with Leanne, carrying June on his back, smiling towards the bright future waiting for the three of them. Life had now given them a timely reprive, and it was up to them to make the most of it.

XIV

Revelations

Leanne was tired. Bored. Sleepy. Victor had recently informed her about his experiences with Schizophrenia. He then set off on a ten-month course in a rehabilation centre. Over the past few weeks, thei only form of communication was throught the old fashioned way of letters.

She couldn't play with June, as she was sleeping. She was also too young to do anything other than sleep and watch TV. An idea occured to Leanne. Victor urged her to open the vault, as he even put his signature on the certified documents.

Leanne snickered to herself. The vault's key was hidden in the power cord of the television all along. She grabbed the key and the documents, and slowly went down to the basement. Leanne sat down, onto the hard, metal floor, wondering about the valuables in the vault. Was it really safe to possess the very thing that had caused them unlimited pain and sorrow to this day?

Without further ado, Leanne inserted the key and the documents in the empty space, which led the vault to slowly release smoke from its corners; the walls closing in contact with the walls, giving way to a huge, huge room.

She walked in, taking a deep breath, unable to absorb the very essence of the beauty that lay inside. Ironically, the vault was deprived of any valubles; the entire area was filled with pictures and toys, which surprisingly held a significant importance in the family's lifestyle.

After six long years, Leanne could finally apprehend the metaphorical words of Gregor Jones.

"It was never about the money." Leanne looked around, as she saw vibrant picture-frames consisting of sweet memories from their past, all documented and protected safely by the vault. Victor's grandad was right all along, as Leanne understood the true meaning of the sudden disclosure.

"He told us to use our memories, wisely", mumbled Leanne. There wasn't a trace of money, in all the pain they had gone through. Gregor had told them to stay together, at all costs. Throughout his life, Gregor was trying to teach them the very importance of family, and that losing one, would have very heartbraking consequences.

At the centre of the vault, was a enormous glass cabinet, in which, was a picture of the same size; a beautiful picture, when the couple had their first walk to the mansion, holding hands. The time when she held Victor's hand, which symbolized the beginning of a new life. A life of ecstasies. She caressed it, and shut her eyes, trying to re-imagine the sequence, one more time.

She walked over towards a pile of stuffed toys, where she recalled that each one, represented a signficant milestone in their lives, considering that they were labeled and stored inside a transparent glass container. Gregor had turned their memories, into a museum of reminiscing.

With tears of joy and surprise, she closed the vault, heading back to the family room, where she gazed, at a humungous framed photo, of the family. She closed her eyes, took a deep breath again, and smiled. Life had now given their family a second chance, and it was up to them, to make the most of every second they had.

As Leanne collapsed onto her leather recliner, listening to a Justin Bieber album, she knew, that no matter what came next, she had someone, to seek refuge in. Someone to protect her from all the nasty evils in the world.

For the first time in her life, she was exhilarated.

Epilogue

[From The Diary Of Leanne Smith]

It has now been over two decades, and the memories of our time remain fresh in my mind. The criminals were punished, and the vault was verified by the law. The false witnesses involved in the case were prosecuted and imprisoned, rightfully. As for Fiona, Victor visits her grave, every year, with a bouquet of dandelions. I'm speculating that some part of his soul, never left her, even if she failed to reciprocate his feelings.

Life, has been wonderful so far. It's truly amazing. Victor and I, are now entering the 50s, and we are happy and healthy. June is now twenty three, and it's rejuvinating to see how mature and talented a person becomes over the years, especially when you're a part of their loved ones.

Sure, hard times may come, but that's where Life is truly experienced. Every family has good and bad days, and every family overcomes their obstacles, with love and care. As time passes, Victor and I are spending some alone time together, our backs rested against the tree, the fresh air around us, the birds chirping, and the sensation of confidence, when one realizes, that they will always have someone, to look out for them. Life is all about togetherness, love, and putting aside your differences, when your dear ones yearn for you the most.

As we grow older, day by day, our bond grows stronger.
Victor has completed his rehabilation course and is now
free of schizophrenia. June has now gotten a degree in
psychology and is now working in a hospital nearby.

As time passes, We have been trying to relax and relive the
sweet moments we had, back in the day. Time is passing,
our hair is turning grey, but that's just what one would call
life. Our family is now free from all cases held against us,
and the guilty have been punished.

Life, is full of adventures, and it has taught me a lesson. No
matter what you go through, someone will be there, to
look after you, and that is exactly what Victor and I have
practised over the years. It is Victor's fiftieth birthday, and
I couldn't be more happier for him.

Everyday, we sit against the tree that brought us together,
with Victor sleeping in my arms, feeling my warmth, till I
peacefully pass away, a happy, proud and successful
woman.